Alice's First Words

By Anna H. Dickson
Illustrated by Anne Gayler

A SESAME STREET/GOLDEN PRESS BOOK
Published by Western Publishing Company, Inc.,
in conjunction with Children's Television Workshop.

©1989 Children's Television Workshop. Sesame Street puppet characters ©1989 Jim Henson Productions, Inc. All rights reserved. Printed in the U.S.A. No part of this book may be reproduced or copied in any form without written permission from the publisher. Sesame Street®, and the Sesame Street Sign®, are trademarks and service marks of Children's Television Workshop. All other trademarks are the property of Western Publishing Company, Inc. Library of Congress Catalog Card Number: 88-51562 ISBN: 0-307-10175-4 (lib. bdg.)

W9-CHC-285

Note to Parents

Alice Snuffleupagus's first words are words your preschooler can enjoy learning, too. Children build their vocabulary through what they see and hear and say. Alice becomes acquainted with some of her new words in the context of her Sesame Street day. She learns other words because they are interesting and fun to say. Encourage your child to echo Alice's words, and look for new words in your own environment.

"Snuffleupagus," says Snuffy.
"Snuffleupagus," says Baby Alice.

Baby Alice Snuffleupagus is learning
her first words on Sesame Street.

"Jump!" says Snuffy.
"Jump!" says Alice.

"Rubber Duck," says Ernie.
"Duck," says Alice.

"Bird," says Bert.
"Bird," says Alice.
Alice likes to say what her friends say.

"Telephone!" calls Grover.
"Telephone!" calls Alice.

"Rabbit!" says the Amazing Mumford.
"Rabbit!" says Baby Alice.

"Swing!" says Big Bird.
"Swing!" says Alice.

"Book?" asks Betty Lou.
"Book!" answers Alice.

"Dinosaur," says Elmo.
"Dinosaur," says Alice.

"Boot!" says Oscar.
"Boot?" says Alice.
Alice likes to do what her friends do.

"Tricycle," says Herry.
"Tricycle!" says Alice.

"Dog!" calls Prairie Dawn.

"Dog!" says Alice.

"Snuffle-ball!" yells Ernie.
"Ball," says Alice.

"Monster!" says Alice.

"Banana?" says Cookie Monster.
"Banana," says Alice.

"Surprise!" cries Aunt Agnes
Snuffleupagus.
"Surprise?" asks Alice.

"Hat!" says Aunt Agnes.
"Hat?" says Alice.

THE END